Fiona's Lace

SIMON & SCHUSTER BOOKS FOR YOUNG READERS • An imprint of Simon & Schuster Children's Publishing Division • 1230 Avenue of the Americas, New York, New York 10020 • Copyright © 2014 by Patricia Polacco • All rights reserved, including the right of reproduction in whole or in part in any form. • SIMON & SCHUSTER BOOKS FOR YOUNG READERS is a trademark of Simon & Schuster, Inc. • For information about special discounts for bulk purchases, please contact Simon & Schuster Special Sales at 1-866-506-1949 or business @simonandschuster.com. • The Simon & Schuster Speakers Bureau can bring authors to your live event. For more information or to book an event, contact the Simon & Schuster Speakers Bureau at 1-866-248-3049 or visit our website at www.simonspeakers.com. • Book design by Laurent Linn • The text for this book is set in Guardi LT Std. • The illustrations for this book are rendered in two and six B pencils and acetone markers. • Manufactured in China • 0614 SCP • 10 9 8 7 6 5 4 3 2 1 • Library of Congress Cataloging-in-Publication Data • Polacco, Patricia, author, illustrator. • Fiona's lace / Patricia Polacco. — First edition. • pages cm • "A Paula Wiseman Book." • Summary: "Fiona and her family moved from Ireland to Chicago to begin a new life. Yet, when the family is struck with misfortune, will Fiona's lace help save them?"— Provided by publisher. • ISBN 978-1-4424-8724-6 (hardcover : alk. paper) — ISBN 978-1-4424-8725-3 (e-book) 1. Irish Americans— Illinois—Chicago—Juvenile fiction. [1. Irish Americans—Fiction. 2. Emigration and immigration—Fiction. 3. Lace and lace making— Fiction. 4. Chicago (Ill.)—History—19th century—Fiction.] I. Title. • PZ7.P75186Fi 2014 • [E]—dc23 • 2012047856

Fiona's Lace

PATRICIA POLACCO

A PAULA WISEMAN BOOK
SIMON & SCHUSTER BOOKS FOR YOUNG READERS
NEW YORK LONDON TORONTO SYDNEY NEW DELHI

For Mick and Annie Hughes
and to brave firefighters everywhere

Many years ago my father's family lived in a small, poor village a few miles from Limerick in Ireland. Everyone in the village depended on the textile mill that was soon to close. Most of the villagers were unsure of their futures. But Glen Kerry was their home and all that any of them had ever known.

My father's great-grandmother Fiona told him later that she and her younger sister, Ailish, used to wait by their front gate almost every day to greet their father as he came home from the mill.

Their mother, Annie, was known far and wide for her hearty soups and lovely bread. Supper in the Hughes household was a celebration of good food! But the best part of supper for Fiona and Ailish was to hear their father, Mick, tell grand stories.

"Da, tell us about how you got Muther to marry you," Fiona whispered.

"Oh yes, Da. Tell us!" Ailish chirped.

Their father's eyes blazed as he began. "Now, ye can believe this, or ye can believe it not," he started. The girls and their mother leaned in.

"Back when your muther and I worked at the textile mill in Limerick, I used to walk by the lace parlor on me way to lunch." He paused. Fiona smiled broadly at Ailish. They knew this story by heart.

"That is when I saw the most beautiful little lass I ever laid eyes on."

"Such talk, Mick. . . . You've been kissin' the Blarney." Their mother blushed.

"So I asked all of the other girls in her parlor where she lived so's I could come a-callin' and spark her. But not one of them would tell me. One day as I left the mill I noticed a lovely little bunch of lace tied to a bush just down the lane. I could see other little bits of lace tied to trees, bushes, front stoops, and lampposts further on. I recognized her lace, so I followed it down the paths and lanes until they stopped just in front of a darlin' little cottage. I looked further on and saw no more of 'em . . . so I knew this was your muther's house."

Fiona and Ailish tittered.

"'Twasn't more than a fortnight that I started courtin' your mum. We were married right here at Saint Timothy's and I brought me bride home to this very house. Carried her over that threshold just there," he said with a sweeping gesture.

"Both you girls were born right here next to the hearth," their mother added.

"To think a trail of lace brought you to our mum," Fiona said dreamily.

Then, just as she did every evening, Fiona ran to get her day's handiwork to show her father. Her mother was teaching her to be a fine lace maker. "Mum showed me her secret runnin' stitch today," Fiona said proudly as she held a small pillow covered with lace in front of her father's face.

"Aye, Fiona, your muther was one of the finest makers of lace in all of Limerick," Father said wistfully as he smiled at her mother.

"Sure the arthritis stopped all that, Mick," Annie said quietly. She tried to smile, but it was heartbreaking to them all that Annie's fingers were swollen from the pain.

"Fiona will be grander than I ever hoped to be. And as soon as she is old enough, we'll take her to the parlor in Limerick and she'll be their best!" Annie crowed proudly as she inspected her daughter's lace.

Times were already hard in all of Ireland, but harder still in Glen Kerry. The mill closed as rumored. It broke many a man and forced families to leave all they knew and seek work elsewhere.

"Where will we go, Mick?" Annie said one day. Her heart was deeply troubled.

One day their neighbor Mrs. O'Flarity spoke to Annie over their back fence.

"My Jocko and I have signed a contract. That's all we had to do to get passage to America!" she said as she hung up her wash.

"A contract to do what?" Annie asked.

"To serve a wealthy family in America. We are going to be in domestic service for them."

"You mean you'll be their maid?" Annie asked.

"Of course, and Jocko will help on the grounds. The wealthy family will pay our way there on a ship. All we have to do is promise to work for them until the passage is paid off!" Mrs. O'Flarity answered.

When Annie told Mick that evening, they stayed up into the wee hours of the night talking about it. Within a week they too went to an agency and signed a contract to work for a family in Chicago, America!

"Chicago, America!" Fiona yelped. Part of her was excited because she'd heard so much about America, but part of her was very sad for she loved her little village.

For the next weeks it was hard for all of them. They had to decide what to take with them and what to leave behind.

The last night they were home Fiona and Ailish put out a bowl of milk for the leprechauns and the wee people, the fairies, as they had done all their lives.

"Fiona, in America servants have servants of their own. The streets are paved with gold and we shall live in a fancy house. If only we could take the wee people to America with us. Do you think we could?" Ailish asked her sister.

"No, Ailish. I think the only place that the wee ones can be happy is here where the woodbine twineth, near the forest . . . here in Glen Kerry," Fiona whispered.

The next morning Fiona's mother and father bade tearful farewells to lifelong friends. After old Mr. Fitzgerald helped them load the last bundle on the wagon, the family climbed aboard.

As they left their homestead and village they all looked back as long as they could. When they crested the hill, their beloved village disappeared behind a grove of trees. Ailish and Fiona cried for miles. So did their mother. Their father just stared off into the distance.

They traveled most of that night and part of the next day. When they arrived in Belfast, they made their way directly to the shipyard to board the steamer that was bound for America.

As the ship pulled away from the docks they took one last longing look at their beloved Ireland. Crossing the Atlantic was long and hard. Almost everyone aboard was seasick and miserable. To pass the time, Fiona made lace—yards and yards of lace.

Finally they neared the harbor in New York. They could hardly wait to set foot on dry land.

When they did, they barely had time to be processed and then make their way directly to the train station to catch the train to Chicago.

On the train there were no bunks or cots to sleep in. They had to take turns sleeping on the hard seats of the coach car.

"At least on the ship we had bunks to sleep in," Annie said wearily.

Days passed. Fiona busied herself making more and more lace. The journey was bumpy, hot, and dusty. They stopped at many towns and cities. Every so many stops they bought bread and cheese.

Finally, one day, the conductor announced that they were approaching Chicago!

"We're here! We're here!" Ailish crowed happily.

The train pulled through what seemed like miles and miles of stockyards full of cattle. They could see a big city, tall buildings off in the distance.

"I'm guessin' the cattle are waitin' to be slaughtered. The Americans eat well. I'll be bound—there must be a joint of beef on every table!" their father sang out.

"Look, Muther, the sea is right next to Chicago. I wonder why the ship didn't bring us right here?" Fiona said.

"That there is Lake Michigan, folks. And it sure does look big enough to be the ocean, don't it?" the conductor said.

At the depot in Chicago there were drivers for hire with wagons to take travelers home. Fiona's father had the address of the rooming house that their employers had arranged.

As they drove through the city Fiona couldn't believe her eyes. Every building was grander than the last—row upon row of them. Elegant people were strolling with arms full of packages.

"Look at those lovely frocks." Annie sighed.

"Made with fine Irish lace, I'll wager," Father added.

"Is this where we are going to be livin'?" Ailish chirped excitedly.

"Our flat is on Dekonen Street. Is that near here?" their father asked the driver.

The driver smiled. "No, sir, we have quite a ways to go," he answered.

The farther they drove, the clearer it became that they were coming into a part of Chicago that wasn't so grand. The streets were crowded with sprookers selling their wares from wagons. The buildings and houses were shabby and run-down.

"This is it—120 Dekonen Street," the driver sang out. Then he helped them unload and lug their belongings up rickety stairs.

"Yoo-hoo, Annie!" It was Mrs. O'Flarity, their neighbor from Glen Kerry. "We work for the same family. They told us you were comin'. I tidied up your flat and made your beds," she called out.

"This must be a mistake, Muther. If you and Da are workin' for fine rich folks, why would they be putting us up in a place like this?" Fiona whispered to her mother.

Annie and the girls cleaned and swept while Father went for supplies. After a good scrubbing, and after they covered the shabby old furniture with throws and quilts they'd brought, the two-room flat was almost livable. They had never seen a place like it. The sink and dry kitchen were in one room, and the other room was crowded with three beds.

Annie and Mrs. O'Flarity worked as kitchen maids for the same family. It took them three trolley rides to get there each day.

"I can't wait for our first pay packet. The girls will be needin' new shoes when they start school," Annie whispered as she scrubbed the floor.

"Pay packet!" Mrs. O'Flarity scoffed. "Don't you know that you won't be getting pay for servin' them? They paid your way here, so every penny that you would earn belongs to them until you repay them!"

"Remember, they are chargin' us rent for the rattrap we live in—they own it! And they'll be levying for your uniform as well," Pert Haggerty, another maid, added.

"But how will we live, then?" Annie muttered.

"You'll have to take second jobs and work in the evenings, darlin'. We all do, you know."

The other maids were quite right. Both Annie and Mick took second jobs—Mick at the slaughterhouse and Annie scrubbing laundry at a downtown hotel. But it wasn't long before Mrs. O'Flarity told Annie about a posh dressmaker in the city. "They are lookin' for to find Irish lace, and your Fiona makes the finest that I've ever seen!" Mrs. O'Flarity crowed.

Annie made an appointment and took Fiona to show her lace to the store's buyers.

Sure enough, they were heartily impressed. They made an offer on the spot to pay a pretty penny for Fiona's lace.

"We'll buy as much as the girl can make!"

When Annie and Fiona got home and told Ailish and Father the news, they decided right then and there to have a party.

"Now we'll be able to save money and buy our own home right here in America!" Annie called out as she danced around the room.

"I know just the place, too. We'll be crossin' that great sea they call Michigan Lake, and we're goin' to buy land . . . ," Father sang out.

"We'll have a sweet farm and maybe some sheep," Ailish cooed.

"What is this place called where we'll be goin', Da?" Fiona asked.

"Michigan!" he crowed as he reached for his tin whistle.

That evening all of their neighbors gathered and sang and danced—some of them even while holding pieces of Fiona's lace.

"To Fiona!" they sang out as they whirled around the room.

"This lass and her lace has saved the Hughes family!" Mrs. O'Flarity called out.

"The Laird bless us all," Annie whispered.

The celebration went on almost until it was time for Mass the next morning.

As the months passed it wasn't long before the Hughes family had put away money in a tea tin on the high shelf in the kitchen. It was the month of October, and All Hallows' Eve would be coming. One night before their father and mother left for their night jobs, Father sat down to tell them a story.

"This is about the Pooka, the ghostly black horse that is harnessed to the Costa Bower, the carriage of death. The Banshee screeches and pounds on the door to collect souls that have passed from this life," Father said as he pretended to shiver.

"I don't want this story, Da. I want to hear about the trail of lace that you took to Mum again!" Ailish insisted.

"Darlin', you know that one by heart!"

"I want to hear it too, Da. I want to hear about Glen Kerry. I miss Ireland!"

Their father obliged them and then he and their mother hugged Fiona and Ailish in for the night.

"Remember, my precious lambs: Keep the Sabbath, love the Laird. It's in your heart home resides, and it will remain there as long as you remember those you love," their mother whispered as they both slipped out the door.

While Ailish slept, Fiona made lace for what seemed like hours. As she looked up to rest her eyes she noticed a light glowing through the window. It was late. What could the light be?

She heard shouting and people running about. Then there was a pounding on the door.

"It's the Banshee . . . comin' for us!" Ailish screamed, waking from a deep sleep.

Then they heard a voice call out, "Fire . . . there's fire . . . run for your lives!"

With that, Fiona dressed Ailish, pulled on their shawls, grabbed the tea tin and her bolt of lace, and ran for the door, pulling her crying sister.

They all but tumbled down the rickety stairs and made for the alley.

There were people everywhere running and screaming. As Fiona looked back down the alley she could see nothing but flames lapping at the sky. It was dark and smoky. Just then a clanging bell, neighing horses, and thundering hoofs rushed by them.

"It's the Pooka and the Costa Bower!" Ailish shrieked.

"No, Ailish, that's the fire wagon. They're comin' to put down the fire," Fiona called out as she pulled her sister along.

"Where are Mum and Da? Where are they? If our house burns down, how will they ever find us?" Ailish sobbed.

Fiona didn't answer. They ran and ran until they tasted blood in the backs of their throats.

"Where are we going, Fiona—where?" Ailish panted.

"We're doublin' back to our house. The fire has already been there and won't be back," Fiona answered urgently.

"How will Mum and Da ever find us?" Ailish sobbed again.

Fiona took out her bolt of lace. Her scissors were still around her neck. She pulled off some lace and started cutting it.

"No, Fiona. Your beautiful lace . . . your lovely lace!" Ailish screamed as she became hysterical.

"Ailish, this is the only way. We'll leave a trail of my lace. That's how Mum and Da will find us!" Fiona said softly, trying to comfort her sister.

Just as Fiona tied her last piece of lace to the doorway of a basement, she and Ailish crawled in.

They huddled there together for hours, through the darkness of the night.

From time to time Fiona thought she heard voices, but then they'd get faint and disappear.

At morning's light, Ailish started to cry again.

"Mum and Da should have found us by now . . . they should have!" she insisted through her sobs.

"The trail of lace will bring them right here to us. I know it, Ailish. I know it!" Fiona tried to comfort her.

"What if they perished in this awful fire? There's nothin' left of Chicago— nothin'!" Ailish sobbed even harder.

It was exactly at that moment they heard a familiar voice . . .

"My lambs . . . my wee little lambs!"

It was their mother. She and their father were both clutching pieces of sooty lace.

"We've been lookin' for hours. We'd almost given up hope," their mother said as she held them close.

"That's when we saw it—the first little glimmer of hope—your lace, Fiona. . . . YOUR LACE TIED TO A LAMPPOST!" their father cried.

"So we followed it. We followed each and every little bundle of it," their mother added.

"And it brought us right to you, my darlings . . . right here to you!" Father said as tears rolled down his cheeks.

"But, Muther, Fiona's lace is ruined. It's covered with smoke and soot," Ailish whispered.

"No, darlin', this is her most beautiful creation—soot and all—for it saved you both . . . and us as well." Their mother cried as she held them close.

"We and generations after us will cherish this lace, Fiona. Always. Always!" their father exclaimed.

*M*ick Hughes was so right. My father's family has, indeed, cherished their pieces of Fiona's lace for so many generations now. Most of the brides in my father's family wore it in their veils or carried it in their bouquets or pinned it next to their hearts on their wedding gowns.

I keep Fiona's lace framed in an honored place in my home. But, actually, it fills a hallowed place in my heart. For every time I walk by it or gaze upon it, I think of my darling